Each Puffin Easy-to-Read book has a color-coded reading level to make book selection easy for parents and children. Because all children are unique in their reading development, Puffin's three levels make it easy for teachers and parents to find the right book to suit each individual child's reading readiness.

Level 1: Short, simple sentences full of word repetition—plus clear visual clues to help children take the first important steps toward reading.

Level 2: More words and longer sentences for children just beginning to read on their own.

Level 3: Lively, fast-paced text—perfect for children who are reading on their own.

"Readers aren't born, they're made.
Desire is planted—planted by
parents who work at it."

—**Jim Trelease**, author of
The Read-Aloud Handbook

D1366565

For A.M.B., again and again

PUFFIN BOOKS
Published by the Penguin Group
Penguin Books USA Inc., 375 Hudson Street, New York, New York 10014, U.S.A.
Penguin Books Ltd, 27 Wrights Lane, London W8 5TZ, England
Penguin Books Australia Ltd, Ringwood, Victoria, Australia
Penguin Books Canada Ltd, 10 Alcorn Avenue, Toronto, Ontario, Canada M4V 3B2
Penguin Books (N.Z.) Ltd, 182–190 Wairau Road, Auckland 10, New Zealand

Penguin Books Ltd, Registered Offices: Harmondsworth, Middlesex, England

First published in the United States of America by Viking Penguin Inc., 1989
Simultaneously published in Puffin Books
Published in a Puffin Easy-to-Read edition, 1994

3 5 7 9 10 8 6 4 2

Text copyright © Harriet Ziefert, 1989
Illustrations copyright © Mavis Smith, 1989
All rights reserved

Library of Congress Catalog Card Number: 88-82400
ISBN 0-14-036885-X

Puffin® and Easy-to-Read® are registered trademarks of Penguin Books USA Inc.
Printed in the United States of America

Reading Level 1.7

Harry Goes To Fun Land

Harriet Ziefert
Pictures by Mavis Smith

PUFFIN BOOKS

Harry went to Fun Land
with his grandpa.

Harry rode
the ferris wheel.
"I'm not scared,"
he said.

Harry rode
the bumper cars.

BUMP!

Harry even rode
the roller coaster.

"I'm not scared," he yelled.

Harry went
into the fun house.
It was dark—very dark.

"I'm not scared," said Harry.

Harry looked into
funny mirrors.

Oh, my!
Oh, gosh!
Oh, no!

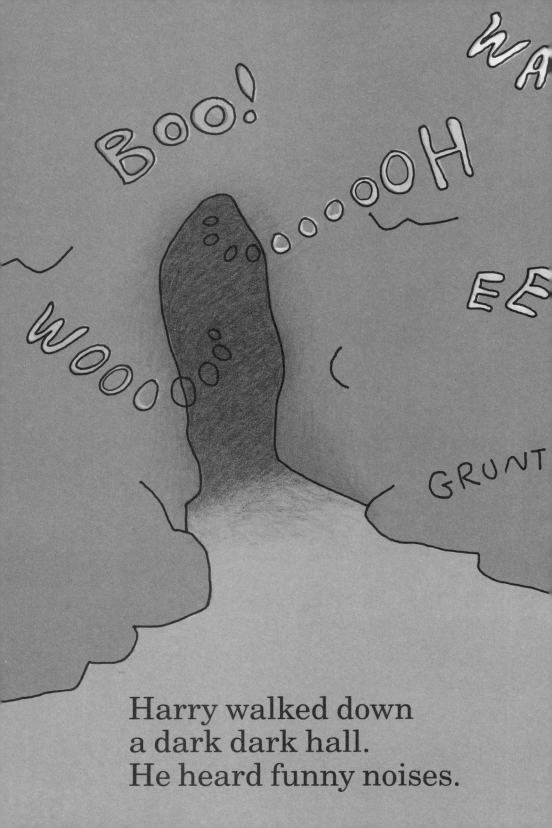

Harry walked down
a dark dark hall.
He heard funny noises.

"I'm not scared,"
said Harry.

Harry rode on
a magic carpet.

Soon he was
out of the dark and...

outside the fun house.

"I'm not scared," said Harry.
"I'm hungry!"

Harry ate popcorn...

and peanuts...

and cotton candy.

"Now I'm thirsty," said Harry.

"Wait here," said Grandpa.
"I'll get you a drink."

Harry sat and waited.

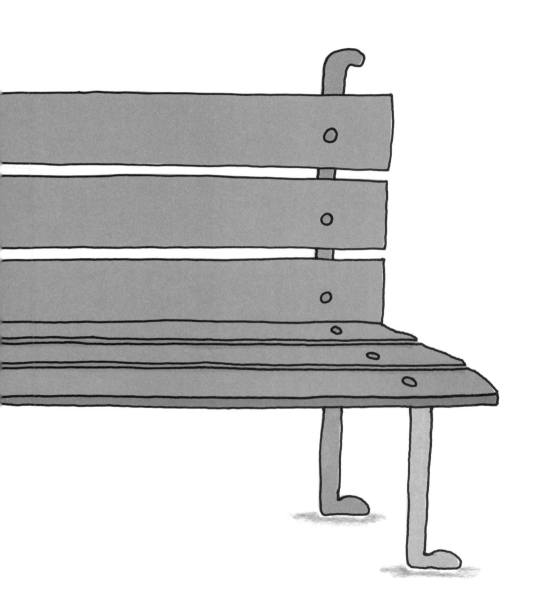

He waited and waited
and waited.

"I'm not scared,"
    said Harry.
"Grandpa will be back soon."

"I'm back!" said Grandpa.
"You weren't scared, were you?"

"Who me? Scared?"
said Harry.
"Not anymore!"